NIGHT OF THE CROWN

HUNTER THOMPSON

PUBLISHED BY

SIGMA'S
BOOKSHELF

MINNETONKA, MN 55305
WWW.SIGMASBOOKSHELF.COM

Night of the Crown by Hunter Thompson

Copyright © 2018 by Sigma's Book Shelf.

Printed in the United States of America

First Printing 2018

ISBN 978-0-9987157-8-0

Chapter One

"And stepping up to the plate is Boston College's finest, number 14... William Hamilton!" The crowd cheered as I stepped up to the plate and got in my batting stance. We were losing to the Syracuse Orange, our rivals, by three points. It was the bottom of the fourth inning, and it wasn't looking too good.

I saw that the first pitch the guy threw at me was slightly outside, so I let it go. The umpire called it ball one. The next one looked okay, but I let it go. The umpire counted it as ball two. The third pitch was straight down the middle, and I swung at it. It didn't go over the fence, but it went through the gap between the shortstop and second baseman to land me a base hit. As Richard Griffiths, my friend, got his turn at the plate, the only thing on my mind was the upcoming Major League Baseball (MLB) draft. The Boston Red Sox had the fourth pick that year, and I was hoping that they'd take me with it. Not that I'm only the fourth best prospect, because I'm the best prospect, but apparently somebody slipped a $20 to ESPN while I wasn't looking.

When I finally zoned back in, the count was 2-2. Thinking the pitcher would throw his go-to 12-6 curveball, and that Rich would hit it, I sagged off the plate a bit. The pitcher had the name "Foster" on the back of his jersey. Foster didn't throw to second base, and he didn't throw a

12-6 curveball. Instead, he jammed a fastball right down the middle, which Richard hit, but it tipped foul. The next pitch Foster threw was indeed his 12-6 curveball, and Richard did indeed hit it. Thinking it would be caught, I tagged up, ready to steal second base. I looked over at my base coach, who nodded. When the pitch was caught, he threw back to Foster, so I jumped and went to second. Foster, however, botched the catch and my third base coach signaled for me to come to third. I ran as fast a I could and slid into third base, safe. However, we had two outs and our next batter was Bill Watson. The problem with Bill was that he thought he was a switch hitter when he was actually right handed. At least he went to the right handed batter's box.

Bill got up and immediately swung at a 12-6 and missed by so much I saw someone in the Syracuse dugout laugh. With his next swing, he timed it better and got it through the gap between the first and second basemen. I was waved on home, and I slid into the pentagon, safe, to make the score 5-3.

I was congratulated as I walked into the dugout. I immediately sat down and noticed someone in the stands by left field looking at me. I don't know how this woman picked me out of the entire crowd, but she was looking at me for about ten straight seconds before turning her gaze back to the game.

I didn't think anything of it. I mean, she was probably happy that I got her team a point. And, we were only down two instead of three at this point.

From the dugout, I saw that our next batter was Sterling Holiday. He is probably our second best batter, behind me of course, but I just saw him look at the ball every time. 0-1. 0-2... 1-2... he never even swung. Finally, he struck out looking at a 4-seam fastball to retire the inning. Strange. We took our mitts and headed out to the field. Me and the first baseman, Jarrod Watkins, were playing catch and warming up our legs.

Jarrod spat out a sunflower seed. "There's someone in the crowd been lookin' at ya for a long while," he said.

"Again?" I asked. I turned around to face the left field stands. Sure enough, there she was staring at me.

"You might want to call security on her, man. I dunno what she's up to, but if this isn't the first time, I wouldn't be silent about it," he said as he threw the ball back to me.

"Eh. Probably just a big fan," I said. I threw the ball back at him.

He shrugged. "Maybe," he said. I thought that it was a good enough explanation. Eventually, this whole back-and-forth thing stopped, as it usually did, because we were about to begin playing defense. We really couldn't let them score. A dude with the number 11 stepped up to bat in a rather open stance. Our pitcher, Shane Miller, threw the first pitch. He let it go and the umpire called strike one. I thought number 11 was going to complain because his mouth dropped open, but he didn't. Shane gave him another hard fastball down the middle, which to my surprise, he hit in the air towards left field. Looking at the ball, my peripheral vision glanced toward that woman who was, sure enough, looking at me again. However, our left fielder caught the ball and my focus was drawn back towards the game.

Next up to bat for the Orange was some jerk who just strutted into his stance, and his jersey wasn't even buttoned. Underneath it was a white shirt that clearly had the logo of the Syracuse Orange. He hit a grounder on his fourth pitch straight towards me. I picked it up and threw it to Jarrod just in time for the umpire to call him out. He blew a bubble, busted it, and returned to the dugout. I thought I heard him whispering something as he went back to the dugout. The umpire didn't do anything though.

Third up for the Orange was probably their best player: Larry Greene, number 20. I had studied enough on this guy to know the pitch was coming straight for Eric Michaelson, our center fielder. I alerted him on this, and sure enough, the pitch went to the warning track before Eric caught it to end the inning 1-2-3. As I ran back with Jarrod, I noticed that old woman staring at me. What did she want? Was she just a fan, or was there something else behind it?

Either way, I wasn't going to worry too much about it. We had a game to win. And, since I wasn't going to be on base for a really long time, I kind of zoned out. That wasn't the greatest idea because my team was still playing a game, but I thought a lot about the MLB draft. Where would I end up, the Portland Sea Dogs? What if I never got past there? And what if I wasn't even drafted by the Red Sox organization at all? I was going to find out all of this in three days when the MLB Draft picks were to be announced. I really wanted to become a member of the Red Sox.

I suddenly awoke to the voice of my coach shouting at me to get on the field. I rushed to put on my mitt, then took a quick look at the scoreboard. Nothing had changed. It was still 5-3. I got out there and threw more balls with Jarrod.

"She still been looking at you, man?" he asked.

"Well, yeah, actually. It's been kind of surprising she can even see me at that distance," I responded. "It's kinda starting to creep me out."

"Call security. Tell 'em to watch her," he said.

"Yeah, probably..." I responded.

"So, how's your future baseball career coming?" he asked. I was glad for the change of topic.

"Uh, I don't really know."

"Have you been working out with some teams?"

"I did do a workout with the Mets."

"Not the Yankees?" he asked.

"No. Heavens, no." Any baseball fan knows that the Red Sox and the Yankees have hated each other for more than a century.

"What about the Red Sox?"

"I'm scheduled to workout with them tomorrow."

"Good. You look good in Red Sox white."

"Thanks…" I didn't want to tell him that white is the same color, no matter whose name you slap on the jersey.

We got the alert from our pitcher to roll the balls back to the dugout. So we did.

First up for the Orange was number 12. This guy clearly didn't know what he was doing, as he swung at the first pitch. I don't know. Maybe that's what they teach you over at Syracuse. Shane gave him a good pitch, and he cracked it to the warning track at right field. I went over to be the cutoff man to our right fielder, but he caught the ball, ruling number 12 out. They put up number 5 next, but he hit a grounder on the first pitch and was ruled out before he got to first.

Next up was number 7. This guy was a leftie, so I caught his last name, "McReynolds." I thought it was really stupid, like this guy was officially sponsored by McDonald's to sell their stuff. Anyway, McReynolds swung at the first pitch again. That's when I knew that it was a Syracuse thing. He didn't swing at the second pitch, and the umpire called it a strike. On his third pitch, the poor guy hit a fly ball right to me which I easily caught to end the inning and head to inning number six. As I ran back to the dugout, I noticed that the strange woman was gone. I found that oddly comforting. She probably didn't even do anything, but I still thought she was creepy. I don't think she meant to come across like that, but she did. Little did I know that woman would soon become significant in my life… for about three days anyway.

Chapter Two

The game was tied 5-5 in the bottom of the 7th, and I was back up to bat in the 9th. With two outs, it was looking like we were going into extra innings. The count was already 1-0, because the first pitch was a little too outside. I stared into the eyes of the pitcher. This was a rivalry bigger than Red Sox/Yankees. Bigger than Celtics/Lakers. This was bigger than them all in that moment because I was a part of it, and I would not let anyone from Syracuse University walk away happy. The pitcher was probably thinking the same about Boston College. But only one side could win, and I wasn't about to let it be them. The pitcher finally let go of the ball after what seemed like an eternity, and it went a tiny bit inside, but I didn't swing. I looked back at the umpire. He called it a strike and everyone in the crowd booed. I knew better than to complain, so I nodded and looked at the pitcher again. He had a cocky smile on his face, and I got angry. I knew I had to remain calm, and just await the pitch. This was, without a doubt, the most intense game of baseball I had ever played in. His third pitch looked good, and I swung at it. I heard nothing but air when I expected it to go back to the warning track. My heart sank. The count was 1-2 with two outs, and I, as the star, was expected to carry this team on my back in moments like this. And I wasn't. The crowd booed again.

I caught the catcher doing something with his right hand, thinking I couldn't see. Not that I knew what it meant, but I got a curveball feeling from it. I was more nervous than ever, and the pitcher knew it. He nodded at the catcher, and the pitch was thrown. Time seemed to slow down. I hesitated for a split second before deciding to swing. Turns out it was a breaking fastball. I made contact, dropped the bat, and never ran faster in my life. The ball had made it through the gap between the first and second basemen, and I had a single. But this game wasn't over yet. I ignored the very loud cheering of the crowd and had only one thought: steal. Richard Griffiths got his turn at the plate again, and as soon as the pitcher let go of the ball, I was off to the races. The catcher caught the ball, and threw to second. My jump off of first base was a little late, but I was still safe. The umpire called it a ball. The crowd cheered again, but if they thought I was done, they clearly didn't know my desire to win. I had two more bases to go. I looked at Rich, who shook his head no, but that meant 'go for it' to the Boston College Eagles. I looked at the Orange dugout and saw that I was now the one with the upper hand. Richard swung and missed the second pitch to tie the count. The pitcher's third pitch was way outside, and that was my golden opportunity. Richard stepped away from the box, and the catcher threw the ball to third. I faked a slide, throwing off the third baseman, then slid the other way to land into third safely. I stood up. I wasn't going a millimeter off this base until Richard hit the ball. The third baseman threw the ball back to the pitcher, who was now clearly nervous. He threw a third ball a bit outside, but not enough warranting a steal home. The Orange sent out a new pitcher, and I knew the Eagles would take a victory after that. He wasn't loosened up at all, and he was left handed. What the Orange didn't know is that Rich hit better against lefties.

"Come on, Rich!" I shouted from my secure position on third base, joining in with the crowd. Rich looked back at me and gave me a cocky smile. He had this in the bag. A 3-1 count? Worst case scenario is he walks and gets Bill Watson up to bat. His first pitch was not a warmup pitch, though. It went straight down the middle and against a guy like Rich, that's not a good idea. He clobbered the ball down the third base line, and the umpire called it fair. I ran and ran and ran. The Orange never had a chance to stop me. As soon as I touched the plate, the game was over and we had won 6-5. The crowd cheered for Rich and I. The pressure was off. We won the game.

Chapter Three

After I had changed back into my street clothes following our 6-5 win over Syracuse, I had noticed that one of my cleats was missing. I walked back to the dugout, but it wasn't there. What that meant was that one of my teammates probably picked it up and that I would receive it at the start of our next practice. On my way back to my dorm, I got that strange feeling that said I was being watched. I blew it off at the time, and decided to focus on baseball. We didn't have another game until Friday, and we didn't have another practice until Thursday. Either way, I checked my e-mail once I got back to my dorm. In the game recap that our coach sent us, there was nothing mentioned about my cleat. I still figured that our coach didn't see it, and that I'd be getting an e-mail from a teammate probably tomorrow. After a quick shower, I hopped into bed until I noticed that a street light was on outside my window. I used this as an excuse to finish my homework late at night. I had knocked out about five pages of math when I heard a knock at my door. Thinking it was Jarrod, or Shane, or Eric, or any other of my teammates, I opened the door to find a girl who probably was no older than I was standing outside of it. She had dark hair, and was wearing a dark red dress that had a pocket in the upper-left portion of it.

"How did you find this address?" I asked in a very serious, yet slightly panicked tone.

"Hi, my name is Moneywag, and there's a dead body in the yard."

"Your name is *what* and there's a *what* outside in my yard?" I asked.

"My name is Moneywag. Well, actually it's 'swag' but with a dollar sign. So, everyone calls me Moneywag. And yeah, there's a dead body in the yard."

"*What?*" I asked. I'd had just about enough of this girl when she told me that she'd bring it over.

I closed the door. Time-wasters. She probably saw our game and thought it would be fun to mess with me.

$wag knocked at the door again.

"Go away!" I yelled.

"Dude, I'm telling you. This guy is dead!"

"What's his *name?*" I chuckled, "Well, whatever it is, please inform his agent about this situation, and *go away!* I'm trying to sleep!"

"Open the door and see for yourself!"

"If I do, will you go away?"

"Sure!"

I opened the door, and- well, she wasn't kidding. That was definitely a dead guy sitting on the steps to my dorm. I couldn't think of anything to say.

"I just thought you should know," she said, and started to leave.

"Wait! Please don't leave! I have so many questions!" I begged.

"But- you told me to leave..." she responded.

"Now I'm telling you I don't want you to leave," I said.

"Make up your mind, uh- what's your name?"

"William. Will Hamilton."

"Okay, Will. What do you want?"

"First of all, how can you be so calm about this?! This guy is *dead* and you're on Twitter!"

"Twitter always makes me calm," $wag replied.

"Can you get off Twitter and call the police?!" I half-yelled.

"Whoa! Calm down. Of course I'll call the police…"

To my surprise, she actually got off of Twitter and called the local police.

"Hi, my name is Moneywag, and I'm calling from the Newton campus at Boston College. There's a dead guy behind the Hardey residence hall." She stood there for a second.

She then put the phone back in her pocket before taking it out again immediately afterwards and opening Twitter.

"They said they'll be here in about five minutes," she said nonchalantly.

"Okay, my next question," I began. "How do I know *you* didn't kill him?"

"I didn't."

"Have you got any proof?"

"Here's what I was doing: I had just finished my astronomy class, and I was walking back to my dorm. That's when I noticed that there was a dead body in your backyard. So, I rang your doorbell."

"Where was your astronomy class?"

"The Smith wing. My dorm is right next to yours, in the Cushing building."

"Why did you decide to walk?"

"Because my brother won't let me borrow his car."

"What's your brother's name?"

"Clifford West." He'd been my favorite actor since I was a little kid.

"Ha, ha, ha," I began, sarcastically. "What is your brother's name?"

"Cliff West. I can prove it. Here's my ID."

She pulled out an ID that said her name was, in fact, $wag West.

"Of course she's being serious…" I muttered to myself. I still didn't buy the fact that she was Clifford's sister, but I didn't say anything.

She put her ID away and asked, "What about you? How do I know you didn't kill him?"

"Because I had a baseball game. We barely edged out the Orange."

"There's a team called the Orange?"

"Yes. The Syracuse Orange. We beat them 6-5 after being down 5-2 at one point."

"Sorry, I don't get sports."

"You don't have to."

"How do I know you didn't kill him?"

"I just told you! I was at a baseball game. We won, I came back, did some homework, and suddenly you show up and tell me there's a dead body in the yard!"

We heard a police siren in the distance.

"Fair enough," she said.

We didn't speak to each other after that until the police had arrived. An officer got out of her car and told us that her name was Officer Drew Kelley. Officer Kelley had long, blond hair to go with her police uniform. She asked to come inside, so I said yes. My computer was still on, and it was still showing a paper I was trying to type up for English class.

"What's this?" Officer Kelley asked.

"It's a paper about the works of H.P. Lovecraft that's due on Friday," I said.

"I see," Officer Kelley said.

I went back to where $wag was, and sure enough I found her taking numerous selfies.

"What are you doing?" I asked.

"I gotta pass the time until the ambulance gets here," she said.

Within the next four or five minutes, sure enough an

ambulance arrived. They took the body away in a body bag and left, leaving Miss Selfie and I.

"I want to know that you didn't kill him," I said once all the dust had settled.

"I want to know the same," she said.

"Do you want to conduct our own search?" I asked. I had never made a worse mistake up to that point.

"Sure…" she said. We both went outside.

Within about ten minutes I had caught her taking selfies. I was using the flashlight on my phone, so I saw her doing crazy poses.

"Hey! West! Cut it out, we're solving a murder here!" I said.

"But Instagram needs to know about this!" she said back.

"Are you kidding me?!" I screamed.

"Jeez," she muttered, and put her phone away.

After another five minutes of silence I found a very sharp stick.

"Hey, West?" I called.

"Actually, my name is $wag with a-"

"Can you come over here for a second?" I asked. There was no way I was calling her $wag.

"Okay," she said. We both bent down to look at the stick.

"No blood," I whispered. I saw a flash of light and tried to grab $wag's phone.

"Dude! It's a selfie!" she said.

"A man is dead and you want to take selfies?!" I screamed again.

"Okay! God…" she muttered.

Stuff like this went on for another twenty minutes before I decided to call it a night.

"Hey, West, I'm gonna go to sleep, okay? I suggest you do the same."

"Actually, my name is-"

"Please go to bed."

"Fine," she said. I walked back to my dorm and fell on my bed. This was not going to go over well with school officials.

As I lied in bed, I thought it was obvious who the killer was. I mean, not only did Madam "West" not care about this dude's dead body, she touched the body. Isn't that tampering with the evidence? She dragged it to the stairs. I don't remember much about 9th grade civics, but I do know that tampering with evidence is a big no-no. I was thinking that I had almost let a murderer into my house…

Chapter Four

The next morning, this entire thing was, of course, all over the school news. No one in the Hardey Residence Hall could go anywhere without someone pointing at you and saying, "killer!" before running away in terror. The entire school has gone into a state of panic. And who can blame them?

Well, like the teachers here would say, "Get back to work." At least I had actually done my calculus homework. I also found it strangely comforting to finally be able to focus on something that wasn't the MLB draft, even if it was a dead guy. How did he die? Was it even a murder? Was it just some drunk guy who passed out behind my residence hall? More importantly, who even was this guy? I'm sure he had some family. Have the police contacted-

"Mister Hamilton?"

"Wha-" I had completely zoned out in calculus.

"Mister Hamilton, you are not going to be able to rely on baseball for the rest of your life. If you want something to fall back on once you are done with baseball, please pay attention."

Believe me, I had tried to pay attention in her class. It wasn't worth it. Where I'm going, the only math I need is the basic math I need to calculate my batting average...

"Mister Hamilton, do your ears need to be checked?"

Well, I didn't want to get kicked out of her class, but

I didn't feel like concentrating. My next class was my favorite here at Boston College: astronomy. And not because of Professor Lynch. I'd take anyone else over her- except maybe my calculus professor. It's definitely not because of the subject either. Astronomy is about as useless to a future MLB star as the 'g' in the word 'lasagna.' It was because of Jake Turner- my girlfriend. She's nice, she's pretty, she's got a great sense of humor, she's got a little bit of everything, and that's why I love her.

The one downside to that is her sister, Rose Turner. There was always something off about her. But I was never quite able to figure out what it was. She's, in a way, almost… too cheerful. She'll look for the positive in everything, and it can get annoying sometimes. One time, I was over at her house in my junior year of high school, and we had just gotten the news that her grandfather died.

Now, anyone (myself included) would have said- well, I don't really have an idea, but Rose wore a smile that day because her train of thought was, "Well, we never really liked him anyway, did we?" and "At least the people he left stuff to in his will are getting something out of this."

I told you. Complete knucklehead. As I left the chamber where what no one would even call a classroom was to go to the Smith Wing where astronomy was taught, I could only think about the guy again. What if they framed whoever Moneywag was for it? What if they framed *me* for it? What would my alibi be? No one saw me between the hours of 8 p.m. and 10 p.m. yesterday.

I figured I'd cross that bridge once I came to it, and finished my walk to the Smith Wing where Jake was already waiting outside.

"Hurry, slowpoke. It's the bottom of the ninth and you're down by 2," she said once she saw me.

"Sorry coach," I responded.

I ran to catch up to her. "You hear about what happened last night?" I asked.

"Yeah, the entire school is panicked about it. That was at your dorm wasn't it?" she asked.

"Yeah, it was. Don't worry though. I'm not a murderer."

"Of course not! At Greycliff, I hear that Robyn and Alex have been coming up with conspiracy theories all day."

"Oh? What are they saying?"

"I don't know. I haven't been over there since I finished French this morning."

Alex and Robyn are her two best friends, by the way. Alex is a very short brunette while Robyn is almost as tall as I am with around the same hair color: jet black.

"When's your next game?" she asked me out of nowhere. We entered the Smith Wing.

"Friday," I said, "but we have a practice on Thursday."

"Who are you playing?"

"I'm not too-"

"KILLER!" I was interrupted by a dude in an aluminum hat with really orange hair. The entire building seemed to stop moving. The dude screamed and ran away from me. College, man. The people you meet here are great. In every sense of the word.

"Uh- I think it was either-"

"IT WAS WILL! I saw him, everyone! He took his cleat and beat a man to death with it, I saw him! I did! With my own two eyes. He ran back to the Chestnut Hill campus!"

Time seemed to stop. I actually *was* being framed right now.

"Hey, why would I do that if I don't even *live* in Chestnut Hill?" I asked the guy.

"So no one would think it was you! But I saw you, I did!"

"Man, let me get to class."

"You see? He can't even deny it. He knows I'm-"

"SHUT UP!" I yelled. I'd had enough of this guy.

"Please- wait, no, please, I don't want to be the next victim-"

"WHO DARE DECLARE ME TO BACK DOWN, VILE HUMAN SCUM?!" I said in a deep, yet obviously sarcastic voice tone. The kid ran away. I started laughing. Poor guy, man.

The Smith Wing just had kind of an "Okay…" moment where no one did anything. After that moment, everyone went back to their usual business.

"Yeah," I said, in between giggles, "it's either going to be the Orange again, or Mississippi."

"Okay," said Jake, and we continued our walk.

On the way, I did think about one thing though. He clearly said that I had beaten someone to death with a cleat. I was missing a cleat. How did he know that? I was starting to get mildly scared. But, I pushed it away and had a decent astronomy class.

Chapter Five

"**M**ajor news coming from Boston College today, as the identity of the man killed and left behind a residence hall there on Monday night has been confirmed. He was 43 year-old Rudy Hayward of Gainesville, Florida. Hayward, who worked for Toys 'R' Us, had traveled to Boston for a retail manager conference. A lot is still unknown, but we have anchor Ian West at the college to provide us with an update of the investigation, and he is joined by Officer Drew Kelley, the chief investigator. Ian?"

"Thanks, Ashley," he said, then immediately turned towards Officer Kelley and said, "Officer Kelley, thank you for joining us. What can you tell us about the deceased?"

"Well, I can't tell you much other than what was already said, but I can tell you that after K-B Toys closed its doors in 2009, Mr. Hayward was employed by Toys 'R' Us. We are currently questioning members of his party that traveled with him to Boston. And we can't tell you much more than that."

"Do you- Can you tell me how he was murdered?"

"Yes, actually I can. When I arrived at the scene, not too far from the body, I found a muddy cleat. There were holes in his body that perfectly resembled the spikes on the bottom of the cleat."

"Were there any witnesses?"

"Two Boston College students found the body."

"Do you know the names of the students?"

"Their names are Kayla West and Will Hamilton."

I jumped at the mention of my name. And the name of Clifford's "sister." I thought her name was $wag or something stupid...

"Will- Hamilton? The Boston College baseball phenom?"

"The same one. He helped us out a lot."

"Can you tell us anything else?"

"I'm afraid I can't, for now. However, I will be returning to Boston College later today to look for more evidence."

"Thank you so much, Officer Kelley. Back to you, Ashley."

"Alright, thanks Ian. More news on that subject coming tonight at eleven. Now, for sports it's time to send it over to Howard. Howard?"

I had almost stopped paying attention, but what Howard had mentioned stopped me dead.

"Thank you, Ashley. On the subject of William Hamilton, the Red Sox had a workout with him earlier this morning. Apparently, they really liked what they saw and are very interested in selecting him with their fourth pick in the upcoming MLB draft."

I couldn't tell you how excited I was to hear that.

At about 5:30, I was sitting on my couch. My couch doubled as my bed in my dorm room. The TV was on because I forgot to turn it off before going to physics class. I immediately turned off the TV to bathe in my success. If I was available at the fourth pick, the Red Sox were going to take me with it! Words couldn't describe my excitement. I was going to suit up in an actual Red Sox uniform, and play actual baseball. Not that the NCAA isn't actual baseball, but I was going to get money. And lots of it.

In the midst of my daydreaming, I didn't hear the knock on the door. Instead, I heard Dave O'Brien calling my name, saying things like, "Hamilton- it's over the wall! Will

Hamilton hits the walk-off to win the World Series for the Red Sox!"

But, I got another knock on the door.

"This is the police! Open up!"

Immediately, I snapped out of it and put on a pair of shorts with "Boston College Athletics" written on it. I opened the door to find none other than Drew Kelley, "$wag," and Rose Turner. None of them looked too happy.

"Rose? What's this?"

"We had the DNA on that cleat scanned."

I didn't say anything, even after a pause when Officer Kelley told me the situation.

"We found your DNA on it."

You should have seen the look on my face. I still didn't say anything.

"We need to question you," Kelley demanded.

"Wait!" I screamed.

"What do you want?" Rose sighed. This is the first time I had ever seen her not happy.

"I have an alibi."

"Your cleat was used to murder someone. Only your DNA was found on this cleat."

That can't be, I thought. I raced through my mind trying to remember everything that had happened that night.

"We had just beaten Syracuse, 6-5, that night. I changed back into my street clothes and noticed that my cleat was gone. So I went back to the dugout, and it wasn't there. I got back here and checked my e-mail to see whether or not one of my teammates had found it. They hadn't. Then this girl shows up and tells me there's a dead body in the yard behind the building."

"Kayla, did you do that?"

"Well- yeah, but-"

Before she could slander me I continued, "I didn't buy

it at first. So, I told her to bring the body to my dorm room. I jokingly told her to do it. I didn't know she was being serious."

"You're saying she touched Mr. Hayward's body?"

"Yes, but I don't-"

"I'm afraid I'm going to have to question both of you."

"Wait! I'm not done-"

"You've had your turn to speak, Hamilton. We'll ask you more when we've got a lie detector hooked up to you."

"I'm telling you, this is all a load of-"

I continued for about ten more seconds, then realized that no one was paying attention. Officer Kelley basically told me that they hadn't accused me of anything yet, but sitting in the back of a police car is still terrifying. When we pulled up to the station, they had me sit down in a weird room and put a lie detector on me.

"Okay, William," Officer Kelley said. "Tell us your side of the story, please."

"Okay, so we had just beat Syracuse, right? I- I went to go change and I noticed one of my cleats was missing. At the time, I figured one of my teammates had probably mistaken it for their own. I assumed it would turn up eventually and I left the locker room and went back home, okay, and I never killed anyone, never touched anyone. I lost possession of that cleat at like 8:30 or something. I don't know. I wasn't keeping track of time. But what I'm trying to say is I didn't kill him. Okay? I didn't kill him! I don't know what else to say!"

"William, please be calm. We need to know where you were at 8:26 p.m. on the night of July 19, 2016."

"I was changing! We just beat the Orange! I've told you that already!"

"Do you know of anyone who can prove that to me, such as a teammate or your coach?"

"No! Who would watch me change? That's so gross-"

"William! Please calm down. We haven't accused you of anything yet. The media doesn't need to know about this. If you can prove your innocence we will have your name cleared. Deal?"

"How am I going to do that?" I asked. I did, however, take comfort in the fact that this detective hadn't told anyone anything yet. I needed to keep my image as clean as possible, so that come Thursday I'd get taken with the Red Sox pick. Plus, it was obvious I was panicking.

"Well, that is something you are going to have to figure out for yourself. Now, I need to question Ms. Kayla West. You are free to go."

I held on to little of that, except the "figure it out yourself" part. The light bulb went off in my head. I was going to ask staffers for security footage to prove my innocence. I was destined to become the next MLB legend, and some random dead dude from Gainesville who got killed by my cleat by some idiot who thought she was Clifford West's sister or whatever was not going to stop me.

Chapter Six

At this point, I was getting desperate. I had asked stadium people for security tapes later the same night that Officer Kelley questioned me, and they weren't doing it very quickly. The date that day was Wednesday the 11th, which meant that a Friday the 13th was coming. After I had finished calculus, I went over to meet up with Jake on the way to astronomy.

"Do you have a suit for the draft yet?" she asked me.

"I was going to go pick one up tonight. Do you want to come with me?"

"Why would I?"

"A second pair of eyes never hurt anyone."

"A second pair of eyes?"

"You come and tell me if the suit looks good on me."

"Oh… yeah. I'll have to tell Robyn and Alex though."

I pulled her off to the side immediately after I saw her sister.

"Hey- Jake, can I be serious for a second?" I said in a half-whisper.

"Sure," Jake said, and straightened out her hair.

"Do you think I killed the guy?"

"Will- I'm going to stick with you through this. We've been together too long for me to not to," she responded.

"Okay, but do you think I killed him?"

"No, Will, I don't think you killed him."

I sighed with relief before Rose walked into our conversation.

"You don't look happy," Jake said.

"How did your interview with the cop go?" Rose asked.

"That's confidential," I said.

"So, did they convict you yet?" Rose asked in a slightly more angry tone than before.

"What kind of question is that?" I asked.

"Come on, William, you can't argue against DNA evidence," Rose said.

"Rose, Jake and I were having a private conversation."

"About what? On where to flee after you're exposed for the murderer you are?"

"Rose, come on. Can we please just get to class?"

"Oh, running away from pressure now, are we?"

"Rose!" Jake yelled.

"And you're an accomplice Jake?"

"Shut up! Can we please just get moving? I didn't do shit! I'm not going to sit here and tell you what you want to hear!"

"Hey, calm down, Will. She's not worth your time," Jake said.

"Not worth your time? I'm your sister, Jake!"

"And you're being annoying!" Jake said.

I pulled Jake back towards class before Rose could respond.

Chapter Seven

I was writing a biochemistry paper later that night when I heard a knock on my door.

"Agh! What now? Did the President wind up dead in the backyard and Adolf Hitler's cousin has come to tell me the news?!" I yelled loudly enough for the person at the door to hear.

"Mister Hamilton, do you recall the tuxedo you rented for Thursday night?"

"Oh- thank God it's you, Jake…"

"Can you let me in?"

"Yeah, one second."

I got up and opened the door. Jake was there holding my tuxedo and wearing a red and white dress, the colors of the Red Sox.

"The tux looks even better with you holding it," I said without inhibition.

"Um… I didn't know I was holding a Linux mascot," Jake said. "Now put it on. We need to practice your reaction when you get drafted."

She came in and I closed the door behind her. I took off my shirt and put the tuxedo shirt and jacket on. Then I went and found a bow tie in my drawer. When I got back to my computer, Jake was making edits to my paper.

"Um…" I started.

"I noticed some factual errors in that. You know Mr. Emerson won't be too happy when he reads it if there are fallacies in it."

"Like what?"

"You don't really digest in your stomach. You digest in your intestines because enzymes called-"

"Yeah, thanks."

"Well- sorry I'm smart, Will. And are you ever going to put those dress pants on? I don't have all night."

"Oh yeah," I said. I started to put the dress pants on before realizing that I hadn't taken off my shorts yet.

"Boy, this whole 'murder' thing surely has you a little wonky," Jake said.

I chuckled. "Can you blame me?" I responded.

"No, not really. But Alex really wanted to show me her child psychology paper tonight, so can you hurry up?"

"Yeah," I said, and left the room walking like a penguin as my pants were only half-on.

After I had put my bow tie and dress pants on, I walked back into the main room where Jake had taken my dinner table and moved it in front of the television. I placed the chairs side-by-side.

"There's the podium," she said, and pointed to the other side of the room. I had sat down when all of a sudden the room started spinning away. Suddenly, there I was in Secaucus. There was a microphone on a stage, and I was sitting at one of many tables. Jake was sitting next to me. I looked up at the podium, heard bells ringing, and saw the MLB Commissioner walk on the stage.

"With the first pick in the MLB Draft, the Minnesota Twins select... Arthur Jones from U.C.L.A.!" A guy near me stood up, hugged someone I can only assume was his mother, and walked up to the MLB Commissioner and shook his hand. The Commissioner had barely started talking again when Secaucus shifted out of view and I was back in my dorm room again.

"Will? Are you okay?"

"Oh, sorry, I was just... daydreaming..."

"Okay, let's run down the list. The draft guy calls your name, you give me a hug, and go walk up to take his Red Sox hat or whatever, and you give a speech about hard work or something-"

"Jake, I'm not going to get a turn to speak," I said.

"Well... fine. Okay, so then you come back and sit by me and we chat about the future and how much money you're going to make once you sign or something, then we get our college credits and we get a nice two or three level house."

"Okay. We can do that, Jake," I said.

"Alright, I'm going to go back to my dorm room now. Don't get that tuxedo dirty," she said. Jake was getting ready to leave when there was a knock on the door.

A voice I have never heard before asked, "Pardon me, but there is a little drizzle outside. Do you mind letting me in?"

Jake opened the door to see an old woman standing outside in a fancy hat and a pink coat covering most of her body. I had seen the woman before, but I couldn't for the life of me remember where.

"I appreciate your hospitality, Mr. Hamilton," she said and walked in.

"Sorry, but- how do you know my name?"

"I've been watching your baseball games, Mr. Hamilton,"

"Please call me William," I said. I was thinking about her in my head, and suddenly it dawned on me. She was the lady who was staring at me during the game where we beat Syracuse earlier this week!

"Hey, ma'am, when Boston College played Syracuse, were you looking at me the entire time?"

"Looking at you- yes, yes I was looking at you. I was hoping you could help me," she said.

"What's your name, ma'am?" Jake asked, trying to change the subject.

"My name is Doctor Cesternino, but you can call me Doc C.," she said.

"Rocky?" Jake asked.

"No, Doc C., but you can call me that if you want to," she said.

"Okay, Doc C., where are you planning to go after I end up kicking you out of my house?" I said, and pointed towards the door.

"William- please, it's raining outside."

"How did you even get here? What do you want?"

"I drove. And I was wondering if you could help me."

"Help you what?"

"Search for evidence on the murder of a Rudy Hayward," she said.

"Ma'am, I mean no disrespect, but the last thing I want is to get wrapped up in this case even more," I said.

"I understand," she said and nodded. "Have a good night."

"You too," Jake said. She left.

"Will, we could do our own search. We'll invite Rose over-"

"Oh, that'd be lovely," I said.

"You don't have to like her, Will, but we need to convince her you're not behind this," she replied. I reluctantly agreed and Rose came over about a half hour later. She also brought $wag with her.

"Hi," was what Rose said when she arrived.

"Hi," Jake and I said back, and we went outside. Rose brought flashlights, and gave one to me. Within twenty minutes I had caught $wag taking more selfies, but I decided to leave it alone this time.

I was looking in the corner of the building connecting

my dorm to someone else's when I found a bloody check. I didn't touch it, because I didn't want to pull a "Miss West," but I called Jake over.

She had gloves on, so she picked it up. Looking over her shoulder, I saw the piece of paper was a check with the name "MR. RUDY HAYWARD" on the front. She turned the check over, and written in blood were the letters 'Q' and 'T'.

"Q.T.?" Rose asked. I didn't realize she was standing behind me.

"Q.T.," Jake confirmed, "But what does it mean?"

"Cutie!" $wag said.

"What?" Jake and I asked simultaneously.

"You guys, the check's calling me cute…" Moneywag said.

"Uh, I hate to burst your bubble, Miss 'I'm-Related-To-Clifford-West,' but I don't think that's what it means," I said.

"I am related to Cliff West… See?" she said, and whipped out her phone, scrolling to an image of her together with Clifford.

"Okay- just because you've met doesn't mean you're related," I said.

"We are related…" she said.

"Can you prove it?" I asked.

"You two, can we please get back to work? This is a huge breakthrough in the case. I'm going to get the police to have the DNA of the blood on the paper scanned, and if they can, we will know before the MLB draft if Will's guilty or not," Rose said.

"Innocent until proven guilty…" I muttered.

"She's not accusing you, she's just saying, Will," Jake said. That gave me a weird sense of comfort. At least for the time being.

Chapter Eight

I eventually called it a night, and Jake and Rose went home. I don't know if Kayla went home at the same time. I still didn't even know who that Cesternino lady was. Not yet anyway. But none of that mattered because the draft was tomorrow.

The next morning, I drove to Secaucus with Jake. We arrived at a Hyatt Place in Secaucus at around 11:30 a.m. The draft didn't start until 5:30 p.m., so we decided to visit a local restaurant. While we were in line, we were treated to the sounds of younger kids screaming. Once we got our first plate it was 2:15 already. Jake ordered tea and water while I got soda and a water.

"Where do you think you're going to end up?" she asked.

"I don't know, but I hope it's the Red Sox," I said. My phone went off. When I checked it, I saw something I didn't want to see. It was an alert from the MLB app saying, "ALERT: Chicago Cubs have traded their fourth overall selection in the upcoming MLB draft for Michael Fernandez and the Arizona Diamondbacks' first round pick via the Yankees."

"Oh," I said.

"What?" Jake asked.

"Some… trade," I said, putting my phone back in my pocket. I looked up at the television again and saw the head-line: "TWINS 'VERY INTERESTED' IN HAMILTON."

That, to me, was heart-sinking. I wanted to play for the Red Sox, not up in Minnesota. I sighed.

"What's wrong?" Jake asked. I pointed up at the television and she read the headline for herself.

"Oh- I'm sorry, Will," she said.

"Nah, not your fault. I guess I'm just..." I sighed again. "I guess I'm just too good," I said, and smiled a little. It was a compliment after all. Just not one I wanted to hear. I was running through my head trying to think if I knew anyone to call who could get me out of this mess. No one came to mind. I didn't have an agent or anything.

"Guess we'll just have to get used to the cold, huh?" Jake said.

"Between you and me, Jake, I'm signing with the Red Sox the first chance I get," I said firmly.

I saw a guy with a jersey that said 'Eagles' and the number 14 walk up to me.

"Hey, William Hamilton! Did you see the new headline?" The dude pointed to the television set.

"Yeah- yeah. I did," I said.

"Sorry man, your hometown team is out of the running. Well, good luck dude! Hey, can I get a picture?"

"Sure," I said. "What's your name?"

"Alvin," he said. "Alvin Levron. Pleasure."

"William Hamilton," I said.

"No need to introduce yourself. You certainly are going to be the best baseball player ever someday. Can you sign my jersey?"

I signed his jersey with a pen he gave me, and then we took a photo. Then he told me that he'd "see me around" and left.

I sat back down, and for a while both Jake and I were silent. There was a TV on in one of the corners of the restaurant and I decided to watch. The sound wasn't on, but there were captions rolling under some footage of me playing baseball. That had always felt weird, seeing myself on television. There it was, again, "TWINS 'VERY INTERESTED' IN HAMILTON." Those words might be the death of me at some point. Jake reminded me that I still had options, and I was going to take them. I was thinking about it even deeper when I was interrupted by a waiter.

"And for you, sir?" he asked. I realized I hadn't looked over the menu at all.

"Uh-" I started, opening the menu. I picked the first thing that looked appetizing: a bacon cheeseburger.

"Can I get the bacon cheeseburger, please?" I asked.

"Absolutely," he said, writing it down. "How would you like the patty done?"

"Well would be great, thanks," I said.

"Okay. I'll be right back with some water for you and I'll get your orders in."

"Great, thanks!" Jake said and smiled. She was always better with people than me. Thinking about that gave me an idea though. I could make Jake my agent. If she wanted the job.

"William Hamilton likes bacon cheeseburgers apparently," said the waiter as he entered the kitchen, talking to someone else. I smiled a little.

"Hey- Jake?"

"Yeah, Will?"

"I just realized that I don't have an agent, and I'm going to need one," I said, a bit quicker than usual.

"How much are you offering me?" asked Jake.

"Enough," I said.

"How much?" Jake persisted, smiling.

"One thousand percent of all my contracts," I said.

"Deal." We shook hands, then laughed.

"But seriously, though, Jake, will you?" I asked.

"Yeah, Will, whatever you need. I'm here for you. I want us to succeed, Willy."

"Please don't call me Willy."

"Then what should I call you?"

"Uh- Supreme Overlord?"

"No."

"Here's your water you guys. Your orders are in, and it should be about 10 to 15 minutes," the waiter interrupted.

"Thanks!" Jake said and smiled. She turned back to me.

"Are you sure you don't like Willy?" she asked.

"Sure, Jacqueline," I said.

"Willy, you're a nutcase."

"I know. Hey Jake-" I started.

"What?" she asked.

"I just… I just wanted to say that, uh… I'd never be here without you and I just… you don't know how much it's meant to me to have you by my side throughout the years. I… you mean the absolute world to me, Jake, and I… I don't know how I can repay you."

"You could call me Supreme Overlord."

"Something else."

"Aww…" she said. I smiled. What did I ever do to deserve her?

Chapter Nine

At 4:50 p.m., we arrived where the draft was taking place: MetLife Stadium. There were tables, chairs, a podium, champagne, loud music, all of the things that make a public place public. Except this wasn't really public. Jake and I sat down, and I was scrolling through my e-mails when I found one from my parents. It said:

"Dear Will: We are saddened by the fact that we cannot be joining you in New Jersey tonight. We here at home hope the Red Sox take you with their pick, as does all of Boston College. No matter what happens tonight, we are unbelievably proud of you and we look forward to your future successes. We love you so much. Mom and Dad."

"Huh. Guess they didn't get the news before they sent that one," I said.

"Will?" Jake asked at around 5 p.m.

"Yeah?" I responded.

"No matter what happens tonight, just know that I love you," she said.

"Jake, I love you too!"

"You'll always be a Red Sox in my heart, Will," she said.

"Uh- thanks," was my reply.

We both stood up and then hugged. All around us we

35

heard people cheering for something. That hug felt like it lasted forever.

We eventually sat down just as the announcer was saying, "Good evening and welcome to the MLB Draft. The picks in this first round were determined by reverse order of the team records from last season. The first selection belongs to the Minnesota Twins, who have five minutes to make their selection. Their time starts now."

"I love you," Jake said.

"I love you too."

"Will- do you think you'll be going to Minnesota?"

"I dunno. The weather up there is frightful, and they already have a young left fielder. But maybe, we'll see."

"Is their future looking bright?" Jake asked.

"Yeah, unlike the weather," I said. Jake giggled.

"You know, it's not so great in Boston either," she said.

"Yeah…"

With two minutes and seventeen seconds left, the Commissioner returned to the podium.

"We have a trade to announce," he said.

"Uh-oh," I whispered loud enough for Jake to hear.

"The Minnesota Twins have traded their pick to the Boston Red Sox for Austin Gonzales and Tony Shannon."

The crowd went nuts. More importantly, Jake and I went nuts.

"I'M GOING TO THE RED SOX!" I yelled so loud I started coughing.

"Will, do I need to get some cough medicine?" Jake asked. I started laughing uncontrollably. "Will… come on, it wasn't that funny."

"The Minnesota Twins' pick now belongs to the Boston Red Sox, who have two minutes and seventeen seconds to make their selection," the Commissioner said and left.

With a flat two minutes on the clock, the Commissioner

came back. A bell sounded, and the Commissioner was reading off a little piece of paper.

"With the first pick in the MLB Draft, the Boston Red Sox select…"

Jake and I held hands tighter than ever.

"William Hamilton from Boston!"

Suddenly, in that moment, I was on top of the world. I didn't know what to say. My smile felt like it was twenty feet long. The only thing I could do was smile, hug Jake, and walk up to the Commissioner who gave me a hat with the Red Sox logo. I shook his hand.

"Welcome to the MLB, William," he said.

"Thanks," was all I could say.

He walked back up to the podium and said, "The next pick belongs to the San Francisco Giants, who have five minutes to make their selection."

I went back down and sat with Jake.

"You did it, Will!" she said.

"Yeah… Yeah, I guess I did…"

Chapter Ten

After a bit of partying at a local pizza place, I was driving back to Boston with Jake when my phone went off.

"Can you answer that, please?" I asked.

"Sure," she said and picked up the phone.

"Hi, this is Jake Turner," Jake said.

"Who is it?" I asked.

"It's Officer Kelley. They need us back in Boston as soon as possible," she said.

"Tell her I'm on my way," I said.

"What do you need us for?" Jake asked. The look on her face told me something wasn't right.

"What is it?" I asked.

"It's Rose. They found your cleat in her dorm room."

"I thought that Kelley had it?"

"Will, you know what this means, right?"

"It was Rose?"

Jake was silent for the rest of the ride. We checked back into the Boston College campus at around 11:45 that night to find Officer Kelley at my dorm room.

"Congrats," Officer Kelley said after a minute or so of silence.

"Thanks," I said.

"Okay, Officer Kelley... where's Rose?" Jake asked.

"We're currently questioning her at the police station," she said.

I put my hand on Jake's back.

"Sorry," I whispered to her.

Suddenly, my door swung open and Cesternino walked in. Jake and I turned around, noticing she was holding my cleat.

"Okay, can I ask you where the hell you found that?" I said.

"Rose Turner gave it to me. Perhaps you know her?"

"How did you get it from Rose Turner?" Officer Kelley asked.

"I told you, ma'am. She gave it to me," Cesternino said.

"I was in last possession of that cleat, ma'am. I appreciate your trying to cover it up, but I am going to have to ask you some questions," Officer Kelley said.

"I have time," Cesternino said.

"I mean at the police headquarters. I believe it also fitting to ask William and Jacqueline to come with us," Officer Kelley responded, and gestured towards us.

"Hamilton, you've dug yourself out of this hole, but please come with me to the police station. Jake, I am sorry about your sister."

So, we drove to the police station, and got there at around 12:30 in the morning. Jake and I got out of my car and heard a bell ringing.

"That can't be good," I said. We tried to go through the main door, but it was locked. We snuck around to the back, and heard muffled shouting. While we were trying to make out what was being said, I felt something in my back. I turned around and saw Cesternino with my cleat. The metal parts were dripping blood.

"Wait, did you just try to kill me?" I asked.

"Keep talking. It buys you some time," she said.

"Time for what?" I asked. She swiped the cleat at me again. I ducked out of the way.

"You know too much about Rudy," she said.

"Listen, I don't know what the hell Rudy had going on, and I'm not going to bleed out from a cleat in the back," I said.

"Oh, you won't. But that's not what I did to Rudy," Cesternino said.

"So you're confessing to the murder?" Jake asked.

"Is that what you want? Yeah, I killed him. So what?" Cesternino said.

"CONFESSION!" Jake screamed.

Cesternino started to run away, but I caught up to her. Eventually, she was out of breath.

"Hey! Where are you going?" I asked. Not exactly to my surprise, she didn't respond. Behind me, I heard a car tires screeching, and eventually I caught the distinct sound of gunfire. It threw me off guard, and I tripped and rolled into a ditch. I could hear the sound fading as I was sitting there, covered in scrapes and bruises. I wanted to get back up, but couldn't. I felt something in my back where the cleat used to be. I thought it was a gunshot, but I realized I was lying on my back. Suddenly, an older, deeper voice said, "Ha," and I heard a gun cock. I wanted to get up, but I was frozen there, slowly dying. The pain in my back had gotten worse.

"Congrats, Hamilton. You'll overtake Len Bias as the best college player to never go pro," the voice said. I looked up, and realized the guy was the same dude who called me out in the hallway that one time. I regained control of my movement, but all I could do was roll around at the bottom of the ditch.

"No, no, Hamilton. This isn't a typical bullet. This one's not going to kill you. It's going to make the pain in your back much, much worse," he said.

I stood up and tried to climb out of the ditch, but it was

no use. There was a pain in my back that shot up through my head and down to my legs, and I fell right back to the bottom.

"You can't resist me, Hamilton. It's what Hayward tried to do, and it killed him much, much faster," the voice said.

I pulled my phone out of my pocket. I had written "HE" to Jake when he shot it out of my hands with a real gun. The smoke lit the grass on fire, but I didn't care. I was stuck. I was going to die at the bottom of a ditch because my cleat had some computer thing on it the guy activated.

After about two or three more minutes of me just rolling, the guy asked, "Any last words? You're taking too long."

"Who the hell are you?" I asked.

The guy chuckled. "Just call me... Aaron Burr," he said. I heard a gunshot and I was out cold. I woke up probably fifteen minutes later after I heard a deep scream getting louder and louder. The guy from earlier fell square on top of me. I shoved him off and saw a hole in his chest. Blood was spewing out.

"Is someone else down there?" a voice that sounded like Jake's asked.

"Jake?" I whispered.

"Anyone? That didn't sound like a natural fall!" the voice said.

"Jake!" I whispered again.

"Okay. Well, at least I won't have to search down there myself!" the voice said again. I knew right then it was Rose Turner, not Jake, who had saved me. What really pissed me off though is that the hole was only around 10 or 15 feet deep.

"Rose?" I said loudly.

"ROSE!" I screamed with all the energy I had left.

"Oh- there is someone down there- William! Sweet Jesus, what happened to you?" she asked.

"You threw a body on top of me!" I said.

"Careful, Will. I didn't kill him. At least I don't think so. And hey, even if I did-"

"Rose, is anyone else with you?"

"Oh, yeah. Officer Kelley and Jake are here too."

"Okay, can you get me out of this ditch? I'm too tired to move," I said.

"Mister Hamilton, please. We will get you out of there," Officer Kelley said.

"Good…" I whispered. My head hit the burned grass right next to the guy's body.

Chapter Eleven

I woke up in my bed at 10 o'clock on what I assumed was the next day. Officer Kelley, Jake, '$wag,' Rose, and someone I had never seen before were there.

"Hey, Will," Jake said. The news was on, covering the scoop. All I caught was, "William Hamilton," "Red Sox," "ditch," and "blood loss."

"Did she... did Cesternino get away?" I asked.

"No, she did not. Mister Hamilton, the Boston Police Department is in your debt for your bravery in the face of danger."

"Who was Cesternino's accomplice?" I asked.

"I will get to that. But I did want to say, Mister Hamilton, we are offering you a medal. We would not have caught on to Cesternino's and King's scheme without you."

"Okay, and who's this?" I asked and pointed to the stranger.

"Hi, William. I'm Jeff Christensen. I work in the front office for the Boston Red Sox, and I've come to offer you a contract," he said and smiled.

"Oh, shit, I don't have a pen," I said.

"No worries, William. I have one for you," he said, smiled, and gave me the pen.

I skimmed over it until I got to the money part. I saw $500,000 per year for two years, with a team option on the third year.

"Okay, I'll sign it," I said. I skimmed to the back, and where it asked for my signature, I wrote my name. I gave the pen and the clipboard the contract sheet was on back to the guy.

"Thanks," I said.

"No, no, William. The Red Sox organization thanks you," he said, smiled, and left. I felt confident knowing that the future was going to be alright.

"Congrats, Will," Jake said and smiled.

"Why is everyone smiling today?" I asked.

"Will, you just blew over a very important decision. It's kind of funny actually," Jake said.

"Oh, shit," I started, realizing that I hadn't even read any part of the contract except the money portion. Everyone laughed. There was a minute of silence.

"If I'm being honest, you guys, I thought I was going to wake up in a hospital," I said.

"We did take you to a hospital. They found you okay," Jake said.

"Well, how long was I out?" I asked.

"About… Well, um,.. Will… you've been gone for about twelve months," Officer Kelley said.

"I- what?" I asked. If I wasn't so tired, I would have been screaming.

"You, don't care?" Rose asked.

"What don't I care about?" I asked.

"Oh, it's funny because we just made that one up," Officer Kelley said.

"You…" I started, but a pain shot through my head. I almost screamed, but I didn't have energy. I started paying attention to the news again.

"Major news again coming from the Boston Red Sox, as rookie superstar left fielder William Hamilton has officially signed with the Red Sox. He is the first player selected during this past Thursday's MLB draft to sign with his team," the announcer said.

"Oh. Yay," I said. I heard my doorbell ring.

"Christ…" I said. Jake answered it. I started to stand up, but Officer Kelley gestured me to sit back down.

"Is… is he okay?" a familiar voice asked. It was a deeper voice that I immediately recognized as my father's. I saw Jake nod, and Dad came into my dorm. My mother followed closely behind.

"Francis- is he awake?" my mom asked.

"He's fine, Andrea. Hey, my boy!" he said and ruffled through my hair. Jake and Rose started laughing. I had a smile on my face.

"Okay, okay, Dad, please," I said and moved his hand out of my hair.

"Are you sure you're okay with all of those bruises young man?" my mom asked.

"Mom, I'm fine, and I'm twenty-one years old now. I'm not young anymore," I said.

"I wish you were though," she whispered.

"Hey son, guess what?" Dad asked after a second of silence.

"What?" I asked, half-expecting him to pull off a mask and say that I was adopted or something. I was too tired to process my environment.

"I bought me and your mom season tickets to Red Sox home games!" he said.

"Aw, thanks, Dad," I said. The doorbell rang. I stood up, but my leg gave out.

"I'll get it," Rose said and skipped to the door. It was Moneywag or whoever. She came in, of course, on her phone.

"William, I heard you got picked in the draft. What's your Twitter handle?" she asked.

"I'm 'bostonwilliam,'" I said.

"Sweet. You have a new follower," she said. Sure enough, my phone buzzed, alerting me that '$wag (@officialmoney-wag)' was now following me.

"Great idea, Kayla. I'm going to follow him too," Officer Kelley said.

"Cool!" Moneywag said.

"Why does she call you Kayla?" Rose asked. I had almost forgotten that she was there.

"It's my middle name," she said and kept scrolling.

"Seriously?" I asked.

"Yep, my full name is Moneywag Kayla West," she said.

"And so you are Clifford West's sister?" I asked.

"Yeah, he's outside right now," she said.

"Bull," I said.

She got off of Twitter and texted someone named 'Cliffy' to 'come in… he doesn't believe us.' The car's engine turned off. I heard footsteps coming from outside, and another ring on the doorbell.

"This is where we bid you all farewell," Officer Kelley said, as she and $wag started to leave.

"Where are you going?" Jake asked.

"We're going to see Toxy," she said.

"Toxy?" I asked.

"Dr. Cesternino's actual name is Toxy," Officer Kelley said.

"And her first name is?" Rose asked.

"Victoria," she said. Jake answered the door, and the guy who I least expected to be there out of everybody in the whole world was there.

"'Sup?" he asked.

"Wait, Officer Kelley… can I come, too?" $wag asked.

"Sure. You too, Will," she said. I turned to Jake, who nodded.

"Nice to meet you, Mr. West," I said. I stood up and left with Officer Kelley, $wag, and Rose. Jake remained inside with Cliff and my parents. On the way out, I saw my dad shake his hand.

Officer Kelley drove us to the police station, and we went inside. Behind plexiglass in an orange jumpsuit with the string 'AA06B411M' was Toxy. She was sitting on a plastic chair. Officer Kelley put a phone to her head. Toxy did the same.

"You can't keep me here for long," she said.

"Why not?" Officer Kelley asked, and motioned Rose, $wag, and I to be quiet. Toxy said something else. Officer Kelley turned to us.

"What's she saying?"

"She's saying she's going to get some friends to break her out," she said.

"Of course…" I muttered.

"Wait, this isn't gonna turn into one of those vague alien stories that poorly sets up a sequel is it?" Jake asked. Rose laughed a little. Officer Kelley shifted her attention back to Toxy. She kept saying things. I couldn't make out what it was, but I wanted to. Officer Kelley had a puzzled look on her face.

"What's going on?" I asked.

"She said 'Yes… Yes, it is I… Queen Victoria the Second, also known as Toxy of the United Kingdom!'" Officer Kelley said. Rose, $wag, and I stared at Toxy.

"How the *hell* did she end up in the United States as a homicidal maniac going after a collegiate baseball player, then?" I asked.

"I'll get answers," Officer Kelley said.

I turned over to $wag and whispered, "I'll admit, I never thought that I'd see the day where I was viewing the Queen of England behind plexiglass."

Officer Kelley went back and forth with Toxy until she sighed and said, "Okay." Officer Kelley turned back to us.

"What?" I asked.

"Okay, here goes. After her crown was overtaken," Officer Kelley started.

"She got booted from the throne?" Rose asked.

"Yes, and I'll admit, she hid it from the press very well," Officer Kelley said.

"Bull," I said.

"I know, I know, but just listen to me," Officer Kelley said firmly. "She got ousted from the throne. She snuck here, and met a guy named Roger King, who developed some tech to make people's muscles and blood vessels hurt. The only catch is… it's only activated by metal," Officer Kelley continued. I stared back at Toxy, who was oddly smiling.

"So she stole my cleat?" I said.

"Yeah, she stole it. She caught a game against the Syracuse Orange, and when you were changing back into your normal clothes she stole your cleat. She put it in Rose's dormitory after following her home one time," Officer Kelley responded.

"Ha. I didn't do it," Rose said.

"Miss Turner, please be quiet," Officer Kelley shushed.

"Sorry," she said.

"Don't be sorry. Just be quiet," Officer Kelley said. Toxy snickered. There was a smile on my face for a split second.

"Do you know of a check with the letters 'Q' and 'T' written in blood on it?" Officer Kelley said, putting the phone back to her ear.

"Sure I do," Toxy said.

"Explain," Officer Kelley responded. She gave the phone to me.

"With his last breath, Rudy Hayward wrote my initials on it in blood. Q… T… Queen Toxy, Victoria the Second. I hope you're all satisfied," Toxy said. I told everyone else what she had said. $wag looked disappointed.

"Have you taken any drugs in the past five days?" I asked while I still had the phone.

"I know they're coming," she said.

"Hey- lady, you tried to kill me. You're not going anywhere," I said.

"Mister Hamilton!" Officer Kelley said.

"Can I ask her one question?!" I asked angrily. Officer Kelley paused, but slowly nodded.

"Okay, lady. I don't know what's goin' on in your head, but I know you know what was happening with that metal thing, and you're gonna tell me about it now."

"Oh- That? That wasn't real. We were relying on the placebo effect the whole time."

"Something was happening in my back that's still itching and it wasn't the result of stupid science," I said, getting more angry with every word I spoke.

"Fine," she said. "Here's the truth. We took some old pieces of metal and put a tiny microchip into them that releases smaller spikes that we added whenever we activated it from our own computer. These popped Rudy's blood vessels, killing him quickly, but with you…"

I glanced over at Officer Kelley. She kept staring at Queen Insanity.

"So then when you found my cleat, you put scrap metal in it?" I asked.

"Yes. When I stabbed you with that cleat, it was putting the metal into your body, but Roger had to activate it first. He never did, presumably because he thought you were already dead."

"Okay, follow-up-" I started, but Officer Kelley interrupted me.

"You've had your time," she said.

"Uh, excuse me? I almost died at the hands of this woman, and dammit I'm going to find out what she did to me!"

I snapped back. The whole room was silent for a second. Officer Kelley didn't do anything, so I continued.

"That gun that wasn't a real gun that the guy pulled on me. Explain it!" I demanded.

"That was the activator he made," the probably-not-Queen answered. I sighed.

"No further questions, Your Honor," I said, and gave the phone back to Officer Kelley, who continued to talk to Toxy.

I decided to leave, as did $wag. Rose stayed. $wag and I walked out of the police station, I guess trying to put the whole thing behind us. We shook hands and parted ways for the last time in a while.

SIGMA'S BOOKSHELF

Sigma's Bookshelf (www.SigmasBookshelf.com) is an independent book publishing company that exclusively publishes the work of teenage authors, who are between the ages of 12 - 19. The company was founded in 2016 by Minnesota teenager Justin M. Anderson, whose first book, *Saving Stripes: A Kitty's Story*, was published when he was 14, and has since sold hundreds of copies.

"I know there are a lot of other teenagers out there who are good writers and deserve to have their work published, but don't have access to the kinds of resources I do. I wanted to help them," he said.

Sigma's Bookshelf is a sponsored project of Springboard for the Arts, a nonprofit arts service organization. Contributions on behalf of Sigma's Bookshelf may be made payable to Springboard for the Arts and are tax deductible to the extent permitted by law. Donations can be made online at www.SigmasBookshelf.com/donate.